BRITISH IN AMERICA

web enhanced at www.inamericabooks.com

MARGARET J. GOLDSTEIN

Lerner Publications Company / Minneapolis

⇨ Current information and statistics quickly become out of date. That's why we developed **www.inamericabooks.com**, a companion website to the **In America** series. The site offers lots of additional information—downloadable photos and maps and up-to-date facts through links to additional websites. Each link has been carefully selected by researchers at Lerner Publishing Group and is regularly reviewed and updated. However, Lerner Publishing Group is not responsible for the accuracy or suitability of material on websites that are not maintained directly by us. It is recommended that students using the Internet be supervised by a parent, a librarian, a teacher, or another adult.

Thanks to Jay Cary, Hugh Elliot, Deborah Robinson, and Jonathan Slator for offering insights into the lives of modern-day British immigrants and British Americans.

A note about spellings: This book preserves the original spelling and punctuation of all historical writings.

Lerner Publications Company
A division of Lerner Publishing Group
241 First Avenue North
Minneapolis, MN 55401 U.S.A.

Website address: www.lernerbooks.com

Library of Congress Cataloging-in-Publication Data

Goldstein, Margaret J.
     British in America / by Margaret J. Goldstein.
         p.   cm. – (In America)
     Includes bibliographical references and index.
     ISBN-13: 978-0-8225-4875-1 (lib. bdg. : alk. paper)
     ISBN-10: 0-8225-4875-5 (lib. bdg. : alk. paper)
     1. British Americans—History—Juvenile literature. 2. Immigrants—United States—History—Juvenile literature. 3. British Americans—Juvenile literature. 4. Immigrants—United States—Juvenile literature. I. Title. II. Series: In America (Minneapolis, Minn.)
     E184.B7G65 2006
     973'.0421–dc22   2005017219

Manufactured in the United States of America
1 2 3 4 5 6 – JR – 11 10 09 08 07 06

CONTENTS

INTRODUCTION

In America, a walk down a city street can seem like a walk through many lands. Grocery stores sell international foods. Shops offer products from around the world. People strolling past may speak foreign languages. This unique blend of cultures is the result of America's history as a nation of immigrants.

Native peoples have lived in North America for centuries. The next settlers were the Vikings. In about A.D. 1000, they sailed from Scandinavia to lands that would become Canada, Greenland, and Iceland. In 1492 the Italian navigator Christopher Columbus landed in the Americas, and more European explorers arrived during the 1500s. In the 1600s, British settlers formed colonies that, after the Revolutionary War (1775–1783), would become the United States. And in the mid-1800s, a great wave of immigration brought millions of new arrivals to the young country.

Immigrants have many different reasons for leaving home. They may leave to escape poverty, war, or harsh governments. They may want better living conditions for themselves and their children. Throughout its history, America has been known as a nation that offers many opportunities. For this reason, many immigrants come to America.

Moving to a new country is not easy. It can mean making a long, difficult journey. It means leaving home and starting over in an unfamiliar place. But it also means using skill, talent, and determination to build a new life. The In America series tells the story of immigration to the United States and the search for fresh beginnings in a new country—in America.

BRITISH IN AMERICA

The modern-day United Kingdom comprises the territories of England, Scotland, Wales, and Northern Ireland. England, Scotland, and Wales share a large island off the western coast of Europe in the Atlantic Ocean. This island is commonly called Britain, or Great Britain. Sometimes people use the name Britain to describe all the United Kingdom. Northern Ireland occupies the northeastern section of Ireland, a small island just west of Great Britain. The two islands, along with a handful of smaller islands to the north and west, are commonly called the British Isles.

In the early 1600s, people from the British Isles began to leave their homes to settle in a continent new to Europeans—North America. Over time, people from many other nations also moved to North America. But because the British carried out the first widespread European settlement of the continent, they created the blueprint for the eventual United States. For example, English—the dominant language of Britain—is the official language of the United States. The U.S. system of law and government is based on British law and government. The nation's founders were mostly British.

According to the 2000 U.S. census, approximately 13 percent of U.S. citizens trace at least some of their ancestors to England, Scotland, Wales, or Northern Ireland. And many Americans who do not know their family histories probably have some British ancestors.

The story of the British in America is a story of hope and despair, joy and tragedy. In many ways, the story of the British in America is the story of the United States itself.

1 FROM ISLAND TO EMPIRE

Ancient evidence, such as tools and weapons, shows that humans have lived on the British Isles for hundreds of thousands of years. The first human inhabitants probably lived in caves. They hunted animals and gathered wild plants for food.

Over the centuries, people on the British Isles developed new skills. They learned how to plant crops and build houses. People gathered together in small settlements. They learned to use metal to make tools and weapons. They formed systems of government and trade. They built forts to defend themselves from enemies.

At various times, people arrived in Britain from other parts of Europe. A group called the Celts arrived from France starting around 500 B.C. They spread their language and religion across the British Isles.

The ancient Romans—who once controlled a vast empire across Europe, North Africa, and the Middle East—invaded the British Isles in 55 B.C. They built roads, forts, and towns, including London in southern England. Roman troops lived among the British Celts. But eventually the Roman Empire weakened. The Romans were unable to protect Britain and other outposts of their empire. Romans troops left Britain in the early A.D. 400s.

After the Romans left, a variety of European tribes invaded Britain. Germanic tribes called Angles and Saxons invaded and then merged into one group called Anglo–Saxons. The Anglo–Saxons took over England. The remaining English Celts fled to Scotland and Wales. Celtic peoples also remained in Ireland.

Also in the A.D. 400s, a missionary (religious teacher) named Patrick converted the Irish Celts to Christianity. Other missionaries converted the Celts in Scotland and Wales. Augustine, a priest, converted the Anglo–Saxons to Christianity in the late 500s. Thus all of the British Isles became Christian lands, with ties to the Roman Catholic Church in Rome, Italy.

The Vikings, who settled in Britain in the mid-800s, were also known as the Norse. In the Old Norse language, **Viking** *means "a pirate raid."*

The next outsiders to arrive in Britain were the Vikings, fierce seagoing raiders from Scandinavia. At first, they attacked British villages and then left. They returned home with stolen goods and British captives. But in the mid–800s, some Vikings began to settle permanently in England and Ireland. The Vikings were warlike and powerful, and for the next two hundred years, they fought Anglo–Saxon kings for

control of England. The Vikings also grappled for power with Celtic kings in Ireland.

In 1066 a French duke named William claimed that he was the rightful king of England. He invaded England and defeated England's King Harold at the Battle of Hastings. William belonged to a group called the Normans. With William's victory, Norman nobles took over the government of England. Gradually, the Normans blended into Anglo–Saxon society. The English language developed from a combination of Anglo–Saxon words and Norman French.

GROWING EMPIRES

English rulers wanted to control all the British Isles. In the 1200s, England conquered Wales. But Ireland and Scotland remained separate kingdoms. Their soldiers frequently clashed with English armies. Eventually, England took control of the Irish government, but Scotland remained independent.

England was focused on its internal problems when an Italian explorer—Christopher Columbus—made a world–changing discovery in 1492. Sailing west from Spain, he arrived in the West Indies—islands off the coast of North America. Columbus had discovered a "New World," which turned out to be a vast landmass containing North, Central, and South America. It was home to millions of Native Americans, whom the Europeans called Indians.

In the following decades, Spain sent explorers, soldiers, and settlers to the New World. Starting in the 1530s, France sent its own expeditions to North America. Under Queen Elizabeth, who took the throne in 1558, England also turned its attention to the New World. In the 1570s, English explorer Francis Drake visited the West Indies and then took a three-year voyage around the world. In the 1580s, Sir Walter Raleigh tried to set up colonies in North America—on land that he called Virginia, in honor of Elizabeth, known as the Virgin Queen. Raleigh's colonies failed, however.

EARLY FAILURES

The first attempts to establish a British colony in the New World failed. Sir Humphrey Gilbert, an English explorer, was determined to find the Northwest Passage—a water route across North America to Asia. He believed that having a British colony on the Atlantic coast would aid in the search for this passage. In the summer of 1578, Gilbert led an expedition to the Carolina coast, but a larger Spanish fleet chased his ships from the area.

Five years later, in 1583, Gilbert set out to found a colony in Newfoundland in modern-day Canada, well north of Spanish interference. Gilbert's ship was lost at sea, however, and the expedition failed.

Walter Raleigh *(right)*, Gilbert's half brother, was eager to carry on Gilbert's activities. In 1584 Queen Elizabeth authorized Raleigh to establish a colony of his own in America. In 1585 and 1586, Raleigh sent two groups of colonists to Roanoke Island off the coast of North Carolina. Both groups quickly abandoned the colony, however.

In May 1587, Raleigh set out to establish a colony along Chesapeake Bay in Virginia. He sent three ships with 150 colonists, including 25 women and children. To equip this expedition, Raleigh spent the last of his personal fortune.

But the captain of the expedition disobeyed Raleigh's orders and landed the colonists on Roanoke Island instead of along

Chesapeake Bay. Then, with two of the three vessels, the captain abandoned the colonists and sailed back to Britain. By the end of August, stores of food and other necessities were exhausted. The leader of the colony, John White, took the remaining ship back to Britain to load up on supplies.

Because of a war between England and Spain, White wasn't able to return to Roanoke until 1590. He arrived to find that the island was deserted, and the settlement was in ruins. From then on, the Roanoke settlement was called the Lost Colony. The fate of the colonists is unknown. Hostile natives may have killed them, or they may have found refuge with a friendly tribe. In fact, some Native Americans in North Carolina believe themselves to be descended from Roanoke colonists who they say intermarried with members of a nearby Native American tribe.

When White returned to Roanoke Island in 1590, the only trace of the colonists was the word Croatoan, *the name of a local Native American tribe, carved on a tree.*

The fur trade industry in North America began in the 1500s, when French explorers offered Native Americans tools, weapons, and other useful instruments to establish friendship. In turn, the Native Americans offered the explorers fur.

As the 1500s came to a close, wealthy English merchants began to seek new places to invest their money. They knew that Spain and France had made large profits from their American expeditions. For example, the Spanish had found vast amounts of gold and silver in Central and South America, and the French had established a profitable fur trade in North America. English merchants also wanted to exploit the vast riches of the New World.

They planned to set up colonies in North America as a base for business operations.

BRITAIN IN 1600

Like most places in Europe, Britain in 1600 was a land of rich and poor. The nobility, or upper classes, owned much of the land in the British Isles. Some British merchants were also rich, having made money from foreign trade. But most ordinary British people were poor.

They worked as servants, manual laborers, or tenant farmers—farmers who grew crops on someone else's land. Skilled craftspeople—weavers, bakers, blacksmiths, tailors, and so on—were somewhat better off than farmers and laborers. They tended to live in cities and towns.

The British economy underwent several changes around 1600. It was a time of inflation, or rising prices, which meant that poor people struggled even more to buy food, clothing, and housing. In

To learn more about the history of the British Isles, check out www.inamericabooks.com for links.

Tailors created and sewed garments for their clients to wear. Tailors were among the working poor in seventeenth-century London.

addition, many landlords switched from farming to raising sheep, to take advantage of high prices for sheep's wool. They turned farmland into sheep pastures and evicted (kicked out) many tenants who had previously farmed the land. Many of these former farmers couldn't find other jobs.

Unemployment soared. Some poor people resorted to stealing or begging to survive. In response, the authorities sent many poor people to prisons or poorhouses (shelters for the poor), which soon became overcrowded.

Meanwhile, England continued its efforts to control all of Britain. It

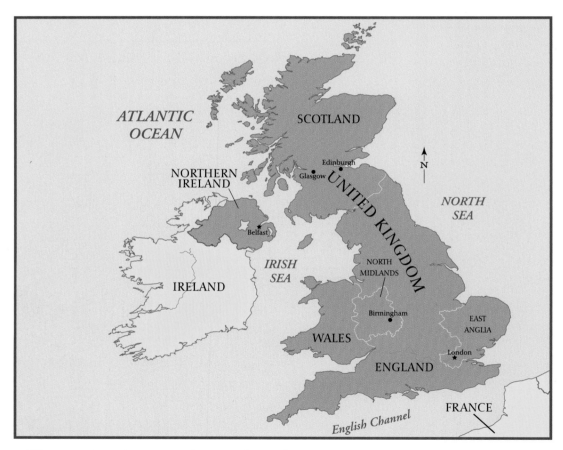

This map shows Britain, or the United Kingdom, as it is in modern times. To download this and other maps, visit www.inamericabooks.com.

tried to increase control in Ireland by granting vast amounts of Irish land to English and Scottish settlers. England strengthened its connections with Scotland when the Scottish king, James VI, inherited the English throne after Elizabeth's death in 1603. He became James I of England and ruled both England and Scotland.

By then England had cut its ties to the Catholic Church. Instead, the government required all English people to join the Church of England, or Anglican Church. But some English people felt that the Anglican Church did not differ enough from the Catholic Church. This group, called the Puritans,

wished to purify the Church of England of many customs and practices handed down from the Catholic faith. A small group of radical Puritans, called Separatists, wanted to establish a new church, separate from the Church of England.

James I was a harsh ruler. He demanded complete loyalty to the Church of England from every English person. He punished Puritan leaders with jail, beatings, and other severe treatment. James especially hated the Separatists and reserved the cruelest treatment for them.

A FOOTHOLD IN AMERICA

In London, England's capital, a small group of wealthy noblemen and merchants formed the London Company in 1606. The company's purpose was to establish a colony in Virginia, rumored to be rich in gold and silver. In December 1606, three ships—*Susan Constant, Godspeed,* and *Discovery*—left England with 105 men and boys on board. The ships reached Cape Henry, Virginia, at the southern entrance to the Chesapeake Bay on May 6, 1607. They continued up the James River (named for King James) for another sixty miles. On May 24, they arrived at a small peninsula, where they made their settlement.

The Jamestown settlement, also named for King James, was beset by troubles. The colonists were eager to look for gold and silver

King James I—like all monarchs at the time—believed that God, rather than the people, gave kings their right to rule.

Life in Jamestown (above) *was not the profitable adventure many colonists had been hoping for. Instead, it was hard work, and many of the first settlers starved to death.*

(which they did not find) but less interested in growing crops. They did not have enough food or clean drinking water. About two-thirds of them quickly died of hunger and disease. The survivors had to contend with attacks from nearby Native Americans.

In 1610 ships arrived with additional settlers and supplies. Gradually, the colonists learned to grow corn as well as tobacco—a crop that proved to be extremely profitable. They made a temporary peace with local Native Americans. More colonists

'Tis for Promotion and
for Honour,
That I must sail upon the
Flood.
I'le venture under
England's Banner;
Although I lose my
dearest Blood:
For unto danger I am no
stranger
When stormy winds
aloud do blow,
I'le not forget thee, my
dearest Betty,
Though I must to
Virginia go.

—"A Voyage to Virginia,"
seventeenth-century
emigration song

small and fragile foothold in America.

In 1620 another group of English settlers arrived in America. Sailing aboard the *Mayflower*, the group included 102 men, women, and children. About forty of them were Puritan Separatists, intent on creating a holy society in the New World.

After a rough voyage and being blown off course, on December 21, 1620, the *Mayflower* anchored on the western shore of Cape Cod Bay in southeastern Massachusetts. Earlier, the English adventurer John Smith had named this region Plymouth (after Plymouth, England), and the settlers chose this name for their colony.

The settlers formed a government and elected John Carver as governor. Like the Jamestown settlers, the Plymouth colonists (later called Pilgrims) faced many hardships. They suffered from hunger, sickness, and harsh weather. About half the colonists died during the winter of 1621.

arrived, lured by the London Company with offers of fifty acres of free land for each settler. By 1619 the colony had about one thousand inhabitants. It set up the House of Burgesses, a lawmaking body. The British had made a

The Puritans who founded the Plymouth Colony (which they spelled Plimouth) in Massachusetts were better known as Pilgrims. They are shown landing in the New World in this illustration.

With help from local Native Americans, however, the Plymouth Colony survived and began to grow. New settlers arrived in late 1621 and more followed. Some settlers spread out from Plymouth and established towns nearby. They made their living by farming and fur trading. By 1630 about fifteen hundred English lived in Plymouth Colony.

COLONISTS AND NATIVE AMERICANS

When Europeans arrived in the late 1400s, millions of Native Americans were living throughout North, South, and Central America. Their ancestors had inhabited the continents for thousand of years. The East Coast of North America was home to more than a half million Indians. They belonged to a variety of groups, including the Massachusett, Pequot, and Wampanoag in the north, the Delaware and Susquehannock in the central region, and the Catawba, Cherokee, and Creek in the south.

At first, Native Americans were welcoming to the European newcomers. At both Jamestown and Plymouth, Native Americans traded with settlers and helped them plant crops. But both Native Americans and colonists wanted the same land, and relations between the two groups grew hostile over time. In Jamestown war broke out between Native Americans and settlers in 1622. The conflict flared on and off for more than twenty years. Hundreds were massacred on both sides.

The Native Americans were at a great disadvantage. For one thing, Europeans arrived in America with diseases such as smallpox and measles. Native Americans had no immunity, or built-in resistance, to such diseases. As white colonies grew, smallpox and other illnesses wiped out entire Native American villages. In warfare the Native Americans also suffered. The settlers' weapons—muskets and pistols—were deadlier and more powerful than the Native Americans' bows, arrows, clubs, and hatchets.

Native Americans (right) *taught early colonists how to plant, grow, and harvest corn. This knowledge helped save lives at both Jamestown and Plymouth.*

Finally, whites gradually outnumbered Native Americans on the East Coast of North America. Assaulted by war and disease, Native American populations steadily decreased, while more and more whites kept arriving from Europe.

Many European settlers viewed Native Americans as godless "savages." They had no respect for the Native Americans' ancient cultures and religious traditions. In Massachusetts Puritan settlers saw it as their duty to convert Native Americans to Christianity. Native people were to be "brought from falsehood to truth, from darkness to light, from the highway of death to the path of life, from superstitious idolatry to sincere Christianity, from the devil to Christ," noted one colonist. In Massachusetts and other colonies, settlers managed to convert some Native Americans to their faith. At the same time, settlers killed thousands of Native Americans, took over their hunting grounds, pressured them to sign unfair treaties (written agreements), and pushed them west from their original homelands.

2 WAVES OF MIGRATION

After the founding of the Jamestown and Plymouth colonies, people from all walks of life and from all parts of Britain came to America. Although the trends can't be put into neat boxes, generally four major waves of migration from Britain to America occurred in the years leading up to the American Revolution and the creation of the United States of America.

THE NEW ENGLAND MIGRATION

The first major wave, lasting from 1629 to 1641, involved mostly Puritans. In England Puritans generally lived in London and East Anglia, a region in eastern England. English Puritans had long been unhappy with the Church of England and the British government. They particularly disliked the king, Charles I (James's son). Like his father before him, Charles persecuted

Puritans. He expelled Puritan ministers from the Church of England and made it a crime to publish Puritan literature. In 1629 Charles disbanded Parliament (England's lawmaking body) and announced that he would rule as he saw fit. This action further angered English Puritans, who believed that the king should share power with a parliament.

Puritanism was a strict religion. It emphasized thrift, hard work, and sacrifice. Many Puritans were unhappy with mainstream English society, viewing it as sinful. Puritans continued to suffer abuse at the hands of Charles. Finally, fed up with their situation in England, Puritan leaders decided to create a new, religious-based society in North America. Led by John Winthrop, they received the king's permission to found a colony in New England (the present-day northeastern United States).

FOR LINKS TO MORE INFORMATION ABOUT THE EARLY COLONISTS, VISIT WWW.INAMERICABOOKS.COM.

They chose Massachusetts (named for the Massachusett tribe) as the site of their colony and named it the Massachusetts Bay Colony. John Winthrop declared that Massachusetts would be a "city upon a hill"—a model and holy society in America based on biblical ideas.

But the reasons for emigration from England were not only religious. In the 1620s and 1630s, East Anglia's long-standing textile industry began to suffer. Weavers, spinners, and other workers in this industry lost their jobs. In addition, crops failed several times,

Settlers arrive at the Massachusetts Bay Colony in the 1630s. During the 1630s and 1640s, the soon bustling colony expanded into a larger area of towns, small farms, and trading posts.

and many people went hungry. Outbreaks of disease also took their toll on the region's population. People faced high taxes, which they resented paying since they disliked the king. For many English Puritans, the new Massachusetts Bay Colony looked like an attractive place to worship freely, to run a small farm or business, and hopefully to prosper.

Most people who moved to Massachusetts were middle class. They were independent farmers, shopkeepers, and craftspeople. Few servants or poor laborers came to Massachusetts. Few nobles did either. The emigrants tended to travel in family groups—

WE SHALL BE AS A CITY UPON A HILL, THE EYES OF ALL PEOPLE ARE UPON US . . . WE SHALL BE MADE A STORY AND A BYWORD THROUGHOUT THE WORLD.

—*John Winthrop, 1630*

parents and children together. The sex ratio—number of males to females—was fairly equal: six males for every four females, meaning that people in the colony had a good chance of getting married and starting a family.

The Puritan emigrants traveled to America in small wooden ships that pitched and churned violently in the wind and ocean waves. The voyage across the Atlantic usually took from eight to twelve weeks. The passengers spent most of their time cold, damp, and crowded below deck with their possessions, including livestock. They ate salted meat and hardtack (hard biscuits) and drank water stored in barrels. The food often spoiled, and some people got sick and died during the voyage.

*There Milk from Springs,
like Rivers flows,
And Honey upon
hawthorn grows;
Hemp, Wood, and Flax,
there grows on trees,
The mould is fat, and
cutts like cheese;
All fruits and herbs
growes in the fields,
Tobacco it good plenty
yields;
And there shall be a
Church most pure,
Where you may find
salvation sure.*

—*"The Summons to Newe England," Great Migration-era song*

LIFE IN COLONIAL NEW ENGLAND

Making its capital on the peninsula of Boston, the new Massachusetts colony struggled with hunger and disease for several years. Some colonists left soon after arriving. But gradually the colonists became firmly established in their new home. Boatloads of new colonists arrived throughout the 1630s. By 1641 about fourteen thousand Puritans had left England for America, in a movement known as the Great Migration.

New England is a cold region, full of hills, forests, and rocky soil. In colonial days, the climate made Massachusetts a fairly healthy place to live, because insects that carried disease did not thrive in the cold weather or the fast-flowing rivers of New England. Compared to other American colonies, people in Massachusetts lived longer and healthier lives. Fewer children died in infancy, and the colony's population grew rapidly.

The colony distributed land by granting a large parcel to each town. Town leaders then granted land to each household, usually from ten to fifty acres, although some holdings were larger. Male property owners met at town meetings and elected local officials. The typical Massachusetts town had a church, a school, and common (shared) land at the center. Many towns (Suffolk, Essex, and Norfolk) were named for the places people had left behind in East Anglia. Other towns (Concord and New Canaan) were named for religious ideals.

New England farmers grew crops such as wheat, rye, corn, potatoes, and beans. They also raised livestock, including cattle, sheep, and pigs. Their farms were family owned and operated, and were generally run without the help of servants, slaves, or tenants (renters). Some colonists worked as carpenters, blacksmiths, shoemakers, merchants, and in other trades. In coastal towns, people fished for cod, shellfish, whales, and other sea animals. The lumber industry thrived in the thick New England forests. Since many people in East Anglia had worked in the textile industry, that industry, too, thrived in Massachusetts.

Most Massachusetts families had six to ten children, frequently named after biblical characters: Sarah, Mary, John, Joseph, and Samuel were popular names. Men and boys generally ran the family farm or business while women and girls took care of the home, gardens, and kitchen. As in Old England, men were the heads of households. They had voting rights and the right to own land. Women could not vote, hold public office, or serve as ministers in a Puritan congregation.

Women in colonial New England were expected to keep the home tidy (as shown in this idealized illustration from a later era), cook meals, and tend the garden. While women toiled in the home, most men toiled outside it, running small businesses or farms.

Social customs were similar to those followed in East Anglia. For instance, Massachusetts colonists built wooden homes, using designs and building techniques brought from East Anglia. Massachusetts colonists also spoke with East Anglian accents (saying *yistidy* for *yesterday* and *glar* for *glare*, for instance). They wore dark, earth-colored clothing made of wool and cotton—and also based on styles common in East Anglia. Men wore leggings, short coats, full-length cloaks, and tall black felt hats (steeple hats). Women typically wore simple dresses, lace caps, and cloaks.

WORD ORIGINS

The following words originated in the south and west of Britain and came to America via Virginia colonists:

flapjack (pancake)
grit (courage)
howdy (hello)
innards (insides)
lick (beat)
moonshine (homemade liquor)
skillet (flying pan)
tarry (stay)
yonder (far away)

The Massachusetts Bay Colony was founded on religious principles. Anyone who settled there had to join a Puritan congregation. Everyone was expected to read the Bible (which led to high literacy rates in the colony). By law, every town had a church, supported by taxes. The law also required townspeople to attend Sunday and midweek worship services. Catholics, Anglicans, Baptists, Jews, and Quakers were not welcome in Massachusetts. Dissenters (people who disagreed with church teachings) could be arrested, beaten, exiled (to other colonies or back to England), or even executed. Only Puritan religious literature was allowed. Colonial leaders worried about witches, sorcerers, and other evil influences, and late in the 1600s, the authorities hanged nineteen suspected witches in the town of Salem.

Puritans frowned on excess and self-indulgence. Church rules

God and the church were the cornerstones of early colonial life. Puritan sermons could last as long as five hours.

prohibited dancing, parties, gambling, feasting, makeup, jewelry, and other frills and decorations. People ate simple, bland foods, such as baked beans, brown bread, and boiled meats. They were solemn in the face of death. They did not hold elaborate funerals but instead conducted simple burials in public cemeteries.

Puritan parents were strict with their children. In the 1640s, the colony passed a law requiring all parents to teach their children to read. The same year, the colony decreed that every town with at least fifty families had to hire a schoolmaster and every town with at least one hundred families had to build a school. Four colleges were founded in New England before the American Revolution.

THE VIRGINIA MIGRATION

As Massachusetts grew and flourished, the Virginia colony around Jamestown continued to struggle. Its population remained very low, and death rates remained high. Men outnumbered women by as many as six to one, so the population didn't grow rapidly as it did in Massachusetts. Ongoing wars with Native Americans made life hazardous for the colonists.

Most of the Virginia colonists (about three–quarters) were indentured servants. These were mostly young, single people who agreed to labor as farmhands (men) or household servants (women) for

This seventeenth-century cookbook illustration shows indentured servants working in their master's kitchen.

terms of four to seven years. In exchange, a master, or boss, provided a ticket across the Atlantic, plus food, clothing, and housing during the indenture, or term of servitude. When the indenture ended, Virginia gave some male servants fifty acres of land. Most people who agreed to indentured servitude were poor and unskilled. They faced a grim future in England, so the prospect of indenture in America seemed like a promising option.

When King Charles made William Berkeley the royal governor of Virginia in 1642, the colony was a dangerous and disorderly place. It had about eight thousand colonists—far fewer than Massachusetts to the north. Berkeley set about building up the colony into a more substantial, law–abiding, and attractive place.

By then the religious and political tables had turned in England. Parliament and the Puritans had grown more powerful, threatening King Charles and his supporters. Starting in 1642, the nation fell into civil war. Many of Charles's supporters, called Cavaliers, fought actively for the king. Other Cavaliers preferred to escape the fighting in England. They realized they could make money in North America, with its many resources and vast amounts of lands.

William Berkeley encouraged many Cavaliers to move to Virginia. He granted them large plantations—farms of hundreds and sometimes thousands of acres—and offices in his colonial government. Due to Berkeley's aggressive recruiting tactics, large numbers of farmers, craftspeople, merchants, and nobles made the trip to Virginia. The colony grew to about forty thousand people over the next thirty-five years.

Although Virginia farmers grew a variety of crops, the most important and profitable was tobacco. Tobacco growers desperately needed laborers, and indentured servants filled only a portion of this need. At first, some landowners attempted to enslave local Native Americans to work as field hands. But captive Native Americans quickly died of disease or escaped into the wilderness rather than live as slaves. Thus, Virginia plantation owners began importing large numbers of captive Africans to work as slaves.

African American slaves process tobacco (background). *To learn more about the history of slavery in the United States, visit www.inamerica books.com for links.*

LIFE IN COLONIAL VIRGINIA

The Cavaliers were Anglicans—loyal members of the Church of England. They came primarily from the south and west of England, where King Charles enjoyed the most support. Like Massachusetts colonists to the north, the Cavaliers brought their traditions and customs with them to America.

In the seventeenth century, southern and western England had great differences between rich and poor. After Berkeley began handing out estates to Cavaliers, the same situation emerged in Virginia. Only 10 percent of adult males owned nearly 70 percent of the land and other wealth in Virginia. The great majority of men—tenant farmers, laborers, servants, and slaves— owned no land at all. (Women were not allowed to own land.) The middle class—craftspeople and farmers with modest amounts of land—was small in colonial Virginia.

Wealthy landowners lived on great estates, with a large brick manor house surrounded by work sheds, gardens, agricultural fields, and the homes (usually crude shacks) of slaves. Extended family was important in colonial Virginia, as it had been in southwestern England. In addition to parents and children, upper-class Virginia households routinely included servants, cousins and other relatives, slaves, and visitors. Children were frequently named for their parents and grandparents. When it came time for marriage, upper-class young people were expected to wed someone of suitable wealth and property. It was not uncommon for first cousins to marry, as had been the custom in England.

Rich Virginians dressed in fine clothing. Silk stockings, scarves, gloves, buckles, satin shirts, lace cuffs, gold buttons, and feathers were all common elements of a Virginia landowner's attire. The poor, meanwhile, generally dressed in patched and tattered clothing made from coarse cloth and leather.

Upper-class pastimes included dancing, playing the fiddle, drinking, horse racing, card playing,

Dancing was an important social skill in colonial Virginia. Dances were good places for wealthy citizens to meet potential spouses.

deer hunting, and fox hunting. Virginians of all backgrounds liked to eat large amounts of meat—beef, venison, chicken, bacon, and ham. Fried and spicy foods were popular. Again, these traditions all arrived from southwestern England.

Not only did the rich own most of the land in Virginia, they also ran the government. Only property owners were allowed to vote (and only men were allowed to own property). Wealthy people kept large libraries, hired private tutors for their children, and often sent their sons to college back in England. But Virginia landowners had no interest in educating common people. In fact, William Berkeley and other nobles believed that education would only inspire the poor to rebel against the rich. As a result, most common people in Virginia did not attend school. Most could not read or write. Slaves were forbidden to learn to read or write, and those who did faced brutal punishments (the amputation of a finger, for instance).

As in Massachusetts, Virginia leaders imposed strict rules about religion. The colonial government required everyone to attend Anglican worship services. Puritans, Quakers, and members of other non-Anglican sects were forbidden to live in the colony, and there were harsh punishments for breaking religious law.

Diseases such as malaria and typhoid flourished in the heat of Virginia. One-third of all babies died before the age of two. Colonial Virginians honored the dead with ornate funerals, marked by feasting, processions (parades), and elaborate mourning clothes. Burials took place at private family plots on farms and plantations.

THE QUAKER MIGRATION

The next large migration from Britain to America was again based on religious persecution. This time, it was the Quakers who faced discrimination. The Quakers, or Religious Society of Friends, were a Christian sect centered in Wales and the nearby North Midlands of England. Quakers embraced a life of simplicity, hard work, pacifism (peace), and religious freedom. They refused to pledge allegiance or pay fees to the Church of England. In response, the authorities jailed, whipped, and fined Quakers for their disobedience.

Led by Quaker activist William Penn, English and Welsh Quakers decided to undertake a religious journey to the New World, where they could create a "holy experiment," in the words of William Penn, and worship as they pleased.

King Charles II gave Penn permission to form a Quaker colony in the Delaware River valley, north of Virginia. Penn's colony was named Pennsylvania (Penn's Woods). Other Quakers moved to the colonies of Delaware, on the western shore of Delaware Bay, and West Jersey (later western New Jersey), just east of Pennsylvania.

From 1675 to 1715, about twenty thousand Quakers moved from Wales and England to the Delaware River valley. Most of these emigrants were members of the lower middle class: farmers, craftspeople, laborers, servants, and shopkeepers. About half traveled to America in family groups. In some of Britain's heavily Quaker areas, nearly whole towns packed up and left. One English nobleman wrote to another: "Many of the [Quakers] and other dissenters . . . have lately gone and are everyday as yet going . . . to transport themselves to an Island in America called West Jersey, and are [daily] followed by others upon the same design."

Then why do we stay,
And make such delay,
When we to a Canaan
are going?
For who stayes behind,
May afterwards find,
That it may cause their
undoing.

—*"The Quakers [Farewell] to*
England Or, the Voyage to
New Jersey," Quaker
migration song

QUAKER AMERICAN LIFE

The lands the Quakers settled were already home to a number of other European immigrants: French, Dutch, German, and Scandinavian people, along with other British settlers. Protestants, Catholics, and Jews all lived in the Delaware Valley. Because the Quakers practiced religious and ethnic tolerance, they set up their new homes peacefully among non-Quakers. William Penn actively encouraged more non-Quakers and non-British to settle in his colony.

The Quakers had friendly relations with the local Native Americans. Penn made a friendship treaty with the Lenape (Delaware) tribe (below) *and paid them for the land King Charles had granted him.*

The Quaker colonists did not clash with local Native Americans as the Massachusetts and Virginia colonists had done. By then most Native nations on the East Coast had been weakened and depleted by disease and warfare with earlier white settlers. The Native Americans the Quakers did meet, the Lenape (or Delaware), were friendly. The Quakers also encountered a moderate climate and a land rich in streams, fertile soil, forests, building stone, and deposits of coal, copper, and iron in their new home. Unlike the early Massachusetts and Virginia colonists, the Quakers did not suffer great hunger, disease, or other hardships when they first arrived in America.

Like the Puritans in Massachusetts, the Quakers named some of their new towns after religious ideals. The name Philadelphia (the Pennsylvania capital from 1683 to 1799) means "brotherly love." The Quakers named other places for their hometowns in England or Wales (Lancaster and Montgomery) or in some cases for individual settlers (Allentown and Harrisburg).

Quaker society was unlike any other in British North America. It had no local militia (citizens' army)—because the Quakers opposed war. The Quakers treated Native Americans as friends rather than enemies. For example, William Penn paid Native Americans fairly for their land and offered refuge to native people fleeing mistreatment in other British colonies. Little violent crime occurred in the Quaker colonies. Women and men were viewed as equals in Quaker worship, and many Quaker women were practicing ministers. Everyone—rich and poor—stood on equal footing in Quaker society. The Quakers never addressed one another as "master," "mistress," or "sir." They called everyone simply "friend." They did not bow, curtsy, or remove their hats as a sign of respect to someone of wealth or status. Instead, they greeted one another with a simple handshake.

Quakers worshipped at simple stone meetinghouses and met for prayer at least once a week. Anyone who felt moved by the spirit of God was welcome to speak at a Quaker meeting. Quakers also met to discuss community and business issues. If a young couple wanted to get married, for instance, they had to seek the approval of community members at a meeting.

People were expected to live pious, godly lives. Parents gave their children religious names such as Grace, Chastity, and Mercy, as well as biblical names, and family names passed down through the generations. Elders commanded great respect in Quaker society. Children were cherished and were rarely physically punished. Families tended to have many children, which contributed to quick population growth in the Quaker colonies.

In Britain as well as America, the Quakers lived simple lives. They dressed in homespun gray woolen clothing. They ate simple meals of porridge, boiled dumplings, boiled puddings, dried beef, and oatcakes. Their houses were clean, spacious, and sparsely furnished. Like the Puritans, the Quakers condemned dancing, feasting, jewelry, and fancy clothing. Gambling on horses, cards, and dice were all forbidden. Quaker funerals were simple, with no ceremonies or ornate clothing.

Quakers valued hard work, which paid off in the New World in business success. In fact, many Quakers became rich in America. Philadelphia became an important financial center, home to successful merchants, bankers, craftspeople, builders, and manufacturers.

Despite their attitudes about equality, many early Quaker colonists, including William Penn, owned slaves. But soon after arriving in the New World, most Quakers changed their views on slavery. In fact, Quakers became the first abolitionists—people to argue for the end of slavery—in the New World. Slaveholding dropped dramatically among Quakers in the first half of the 1700s, and Quakers took the lead in the American antislavery movement.

THE BACKCOUNTRY MIGRATION

The last major British migration to the New World was a large one. Between 1717 and 1775, about 275,000 British people left their homes for America. About 75,000 of them came from Scotland. Another 50,000 came from the far north of England. But the majority—about 150,000—came from Northern Ireland. At the time, Northern Ireland was home to many English and Scottish people whose ancestors had received Irish land from King James in the early 1600s. The northern Irish immigrants were called Scots-Irish, although many of them had English, not Scottish, ancestors.

Unlike the Puritans and Quakers, this last wave of British immigrants did not leave home due to religious persecution. Instead, they came to better their lives and economic prospects. Life in Scotland, Northern Ireland, and the north of England was difficult in the eighteenth century. Rents were high, wages were low, and taxes were heavy. People suffered crop failures, food shortages, and outbreaks of disease. In Northern Ireland, the linen industry, on which many people relied for their living, fell on hard times in the 1700s.

All of northern Britain—

especially Scotland—was a rugged and sometimes lawless country, and the northern British immigrants were a little rough around the edges. They were generally poor or middle class. They were independent minded and tended to distrust authority, such as the king and organized government. Most Scottish and Scots-Irish immigrants belonged to the Presbyterian Church. They were somewhat evangelical, or passionate, in their religious beliefs.

Most people in this migration headed out for America in family groups. Sometimes whole neighborhoods traveled together. According to English writer Samuel Johnson, this sort of group migration eased the transition to new surroundings. "He that goes thus accompanied," Johnson explained, ". . . sits down in a better climate, surrounded by his kindred and his friends: they carry with them their language, their opinions, their popular songs and hereditary merriment: they change nothing but the place of their abode."

BRITISH DIVERSITY

In some ways, English, Scottish, Scots-Irish, and Welsh immigrants to North American had very similar backgrounds. Most were Protestants, although they belonged to different sects beneath the Protestant umbrella. They shared a common language—English. They were all British citizens and had lived near one another on the islands that made up Great Britain.

But the migrants were still diverse. For instance, the Welsh and Scottish had their own songs, customs, stories, foods, and ways of dress. Many Welsh migrants spoke Welsh, the ancient language of Wales, in addition to English. Many Scottish migrants spoke Scottish Gaelic, Scotland's traditional language.

In America Welsh, Scottish, and Scots-Irish migrants usually blended in easily with the English population. But they also banded together to preserve their heritage. For instance, many Scottish Americans formed Scottish social clubs called Saint Andrew's societies. Many Welsh Americans lived near one another in all-Welsh communities, such as Cambria in western Pennsylvania.

As earlier immigrants had, the northern British migrants packed into crowded ships for the voyage across the Atlantic. By then—due to better ships and navigation techniques—the voyage took only about six weeks. Most arrived at Philadelphia and nearby ports. They frequently shocked the pious, soft-spoken Quakers there with their rough and disorderly conduct.

Although not impressed by the raucous newcomers, Quaker leaders thought they might serve as a useful buffer, or shield, against unfriendly Native Americans to the west and south. Colonial leaders encouraged the new immigrants to head to the Pennsylvania backcountry, or frontier. They fanned out into western Pennsylvania, Maryland, Georgia, Kentucky, Tennessee, Virginia, and the Carolinas.

CONVICT COLONISTS

Starting in 1717, the British government began sending convicted felons to the American colonies instead of jailing or executing them. (The government also sent beggars, orphans, and other "undesirables" to America.) In America convicts worked as indentured servants, usually with terms of fourteen years. Between 1718 and 1775, about fifty thousand felons went to America. Most were young, unmarried men, and most went to Virginia or Maryland, where they worked as tobacco field hands. After the start of the American Revolution in 1775, the British government began sending convicts to Australia instead of America.

BACKCOUNTRY LIFE

The northern British immigrants established small settlements, scattered throughout the hills and hollows of the backcountry. They named places after their homes in Britain (Cumberland), after individual families (Knoxville), and after the hardships they faced in the wilderness (Hardbargain Branch).

Extended families (cousins, aunts, uncles, and so on) often settled near one another in the backcountry. Family members showed great loyalty to one another and tended to be suspicious of outsiders, as they had been in northern Britain. Backcountry settlers often married within the family—taking first and second cousins as husbands and wives. Young people usually married in their teens, and families had five to ten children on average. Wives were expected to obey their husbands.

As earlier colonists had done, the northern British migrants brought their folkways—their ballads, stories, folk medicines, speech patterns, and other traditions—with them to America. They ate the same kinds of foods they had enjoyed in Britain, including potatoes, bacon, griddle cakes, corn mush, and corn bread. Whiskey had been a favorite drink in northern Britain, and its popularity continued in America.

The camp meeting, or outdoor religious meeting, had been a common event in northern Britain. In America the tradition remained. Religious people

gathered outdoors for many days of preaching, praying, shouting, and singing. Along with Christian principles, many people believed in magic, witchcraft, wizardry, and astrology.

The backcountry settlers generally worked as farmers, growing crops and raising livestock. Most of them were tenant farmers. They wove their own clothes out of linsey-woolsey—a sturdy combination of wool and linen or cotton. Their homes were simple log cabins, usually with a single room and a dirt floor.

The remote backcountry had few formal schools, and many residents could not read or write. Although

Camp meetings, also known as revivals, lasted several days. They were meant to renew religious fervor, not to replace regular church activities.

44

they didn't greatly value education, the backcountry settlers did establish several academies to prepare young men to become ministers.

The backcountry settlers enjoyed themselves with drinking, dancing, and fiddle playing, especially at happy occasions such as weddings. They liked sports and games, especially wrestling, track–and–field contests, and shooting—all pastimes that had been popular in northern Britain.

The frontier could be lawless and violent, and life was harsh for settlers. Clashes with local Native Americans were common. Settlers often took the law into their own hands. Rather than wait for a sheriff to arrest a criminal, vigilantes (volunteer crime fighters) often pursued and punished wrongdoers on their own.

Dancing to the fiddle was a favorite pastime of the backcountry settlers.

3 ANGLO-AMERICA

By 1733 the British had established thirteen colonies along the Atlantic coast of North America. These colonies were Connecticut, Massachusetts, New Hampshire, and Rhode Island in New England; Delaware, New Jersey, New York, and Pennsylvania in the mid-Atlantic region; Maryland and Virginia around the Chesapeake Bay; and Georgia, North Carolina, and South Carolina in the South.

British settlers also kept spreading farther out into the frontier—crossing the Appalachian Mountains into Tennessee and Kentucky, for instance. Meanwhile, France and Spain controlled other parts of North America. France held eastern Canada and lands around the Mississippi River. Spain held Florida, the American Southwest, and islands in the Caribbean Sea. In a conflict called the French and Indian War (1754–1763), the British and the

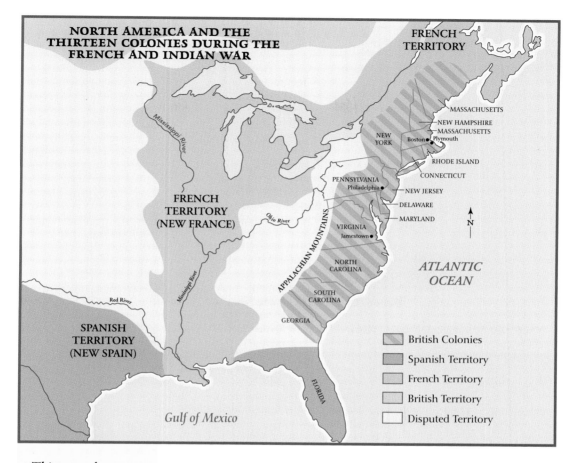

NORTH AMERICA AND THE THIRTEEN COLONIES DURING THE FRENCH AND INDIAN WAR

FRENCH TERRITORY

FRENCH TERRITORY (NEW FRANCE)

SPANISH TERRITORY (NEW SPAIN)

Mississippi River

Ohio River

Red River

Mississippi River

Appalachian Mountains

MASSACHUSETTS
NEW HAMPSHIRE
MASSACHUSETTS
NEW YORK
Boston ● Plymouth
RHODE ISLAND
CONNECTICUT
PENNSYLVANIA
Philadelphia ●
NEW JERSEY
DELAWARE
MARYLAND
VIRGINIA
Jamestown ●
NORTH CAROLINA
SOUTH CAROLINA
GEORGIA
FLORIDA

ATLANTIC OCEAN

N

Gulf of Mexico

British Colonies
Spanish Territory
French Territory
British Territory
Disputed Territory

This map shows the thirteen English colonies in North America and the European territories that were the subject of the French and Indian War. Visit www.inamericabooks.com to download this and other maps.

French fought over control of North American territory. Britain prevailed and took over French territory, from eastern Canada, west to the Mississippi River, and south to Louisiana. The British also acquired Florida from Spain at the war's end.

THE NEW UNITED STATES

The British in North America governed themselves through elected and appointed officials and bodies such as town councils and colonial legislatures (lawmaking bodies). Qualifications for voting varied among the colonies, but generally only white, male property owners were eligible to vote. But Britain still held ultimate authority over its North American colonies. It stationed groups of soldiers in North America. The king appointed some colonial officials. Parliament passed some laws for the colonies and had the power to overturn laws passed by colonial legislatures. Britain also taxed the colonists.

By the 1770s, the colonists had grown unhappy with British rule. To free themselves of Great Britain, they fought the American Revolution. During the war, they created the United States of

British soldiers (in red uniforms) *fought hard to crush the rebellion of the thirteen American colonies, but ultimately they failed.*

CHECK OUT
WWW.INAMERICABOOKS.COM
FOR LINKS TO MORE
INFORMATION ABOUT THE
AMERICAN REVOLUTION.

America, a new nation based on democratic principles (government by the people).

About 77 percent of the white population of the new United States had roots in Britain. In addition, Indian, African, Scandinavian, Dutch, German, French, and other peoples lived in the new country. They, too, had brought their cultural traditions to America. But because the British were the largest and most powerful group, they set the overall tone for the nation's social and cultural life. For example, English, the language of the British colonists, was the new nation's official language. The legal and governing systems set up after independence were modeled on British systems. Most leaders of the new country—including George Washington, Benjamin Franklin, and John Adams—traced their ancestors to Britain.

Although many Puritan, Quaker, and other traditions remained in the new United States, certain traditions of the first settlers were cast aside. For instance, while Massachusetts and other colonies had placed religious restrictions on citizens, the U.S. Constitution established freedom of religion and the separation of church and state. That meant that people in the United States were free to worship as they chose, that the nation had no official religion, and that government and religious groups operated entirely independent of each other. Catholics, Jews, and others all lived in the young United States, but most citizens were Protestants.

THE ANGLO MAINSTREAM

The United States continued to expand westward, to the Great Plains, the Rocky Mountains, and beyond. With its vast amounts of land and resources and its principles of religious freedom and democracy, the young United States was attractive to immigrants. Many still came from Britain. Like many earlier British immigrants to America, they came to escape poverty at home. Because they spoke English and shared many customs with U.S. citizens, they blended easily into U.S. society.

In the 1840s, hundreds of thousands of Irish people came to the United States to escape famine in their nation. Later in the 1800s, millions of immigrants arrived from Poland, Russia, Czechoslovakia, Hungary, Greece, Italy, China, Japan, and other countries. Many of the new arrivals practiced Catholicism, Judaism, or Asian religions. Except for the Irish, most didn't speak English. Their foods, dress, and customs were unfamiliar to Anglo-Americans (Americans of British descent). Some Anglo-Americans didn't like or trust the new immigrants, whom they viewed as unwelcome outsiders.

At the same time, more British immigrants came to the United States—again driven by poverty and hardship at home. In the United States, they found work in factories and mills, and on railroads and construction sites. Some bought farmland in the middle or western United States.

> *Notice!—1851*
> *EMIGRATION TO NEW YORK AND QUEBEC*
> *By regular First Class Packet Ships*
> *The well known First Class*
> *Favorite Passenger Ship JOHN,*
> *Will be [dispatched] from Plymouth to New York direct, on or about the 25th of March.*
>
> *—nineteenth-century British advertisement*

SALES TACTICS

In the late 1800s, U.S. railroad companies were laying tracks across the American West. To make their rail lines profitable, the companies needed people to settle near the tracks and build towns and farms. Using professional advertising techniques, railroad companies printed posters *(right)*, pamphlets, and other documents offering land for sale in the United States, then distributed the materials in Britain. The companies promised low-interest loans to British immigrants who wanted to buy land. Thousands of British farmers and laborers responded to the advertising campaign and moved to the American West in the late 1800s.

RICH FARMING LANDS!

ON THE LINE OF THE

Union Pacific Railroad!

Located in the GREAT CENTRAL BELT of POPU-
LATION, COMMERCE and WEALTH, and
adjoining the WORLD'S HIGHWAY
from OCEAN TO OCEAN.

12,000,000 ACRES!

*3,000,000 Acres in Central and
Eastern Nebraska, in the Platte Valley, now for sale!*

We invite the attention of all parties seeking
a HOME, to the LANDS offered for sale by this Company.

The Vast Quantity of Land from which to select, enables every one to secure such a location as he desires, suitable to any branch of farming or stock raising.

The Prices are Extremely Low. The amount of land owned by the Company is so large that they are determined to sell at the cheapest possible rates, ranging from $1.50 to $8.00 per acre.

The Terms of Payment are Easy. Ten years' credit at six per cent interest. A deduction of ten per cent for cash.

The Location is Central, along the 41st parallel, the favorite latitude of America. Equally well adapted to corn or wheat; free from the long, cold winters of the Northern, and the hot, unhealthy influences of the Southern States.

The Face of the Country is diversified with hill and dale, grain land and meadow, rich bottoms, low bluffs, and undulating tables, all covered with a thick growth of sweet nutritious grasses.

The Soil is a dark loam, slightly impregnated with lime, free from stone and gravel, and eminently adapted to grass, grain and root crops; the subsoil is usually light and porous, retaining moisture with wonderful tenacity.

The Climate is mild and healthful; the atmosphere dry and pure. Epidemic diseases never prevail; Fever and Ague are unknown. The greatest amount of rain falls between March and October. The Winters are dry with but little snow.

The Productions are wheat, corn, oats, barley, rye and root crops, and vegetables generally. Flax, sweet potatoes, sorghum, etc., etc., do well and yield largely.

Fruits, both Wild and Cultivated, do remarkably well. The freedom from frosts in May and September, in connection with the dry Winters and warm soil, renders this State eminently adapted to fruit culture.

Stock Raising in all its branches, is particularly profitable on the wide ranges of rich pasturage. Cattle and sheep feed with avidity and fatten upon the nutritious grasses without grain; hogs thrive well, and wool growing is exceedingly remunerative.

Timber is found on the streams and grows rapidly.

Coal of excellent quality, exists in vast quantities on the line of the road in Wyoming, and is furnished to settlers at reduced rates.

Market Facilities are the best in the West; the great mining regions of Wyoming, Colorado, Utah and Nevada, are supplied by the farmers of Platte Valley.

The Title given the purchaser is absolute, in fee simple, and free from all incumbrances, derived directly from the United States.

Soldiers of the Late War are entitled to a Homestead of one hundred and sixty acres, within Railroad limits, which is equal to a bounty of $400.

Persons of Foreign Birth are also entitled to the benefits of the Free Homestead Law, on declaring their intentions of becoming citizens of the United States; this they may do immediately on their arrival in this country.

For Colonies, the lands on the line of the Union Pacific Railroad afford the *best locations* in the West.

TOWN LOTS FOR SALE VERY CHEAP in the most important towns on the line of the Road, affording excellent opportunities for business or investments.

Full information in regard to lands, prices, terms of sale, &c., together with pamphlets, circulars and maps, may be obtained from all the Agents of the Department, also the

"PIONEER."

A handsome ILLUSTRATED PAPER, with maps, etc., and containing the HOMESTEAD LAW. *Mailed free* to all applicants. Address

O. F. DAVIS,
Land Commissioner, U. P. R. R.
OMAHA, NEB.

The British immigrants fit easily into U.S. society and rarely faced the sort of hostility experienced by other immigrants.

As the United States became more and more diverse, people of British descent tried to promote and preserve their own heritage. For instance, in

1890 a group of Anglo–American women founded the Daughters of the American Revolution, a patriotic society for women who can trace their ancestry to someone involved in the fight for U.S. independence. In 1897 people in Plymouth, Massachusetts, founded the Mayflower Society—for those who can trace their ancestry to one of the 102 passengers aboard the *Mayflower*. The Welcome Society of Pennsylvania formed in 1906 to honor the Quakers who came to America with William Penn. Scottish Americans and Welsh Americans formed their own heritage groups. Especially in the eastern United States, some families boasted proudly of their colonial ancestors. They passed down family names from one generation to the next. They kept careful track of their genealogies, or family trees.

ALLIES

In 1914 World War I broke out in Europe. On one side were the Central powers, led by Germany and Austria–Hungary. On the other side were the Allied powers, led by Great Britain, France, and Russia. The United States joined the Allied powers in 1917 and helped them win the war. This alliance strengthened ties between the United States and Great Britain.

A few decades later, another war (World War II, 1939–1945) broke out in Europe. Once more, the United States assisted Great Britain and its allies. After the war, some U.S. soldiers married women they had met while stationed in Britain. They brought these war brides home to live in the United States.

MANY PEOPLE ARE INTERESTED IN LEARNING ABOUT THEIR FAMILY'S HISTORY. THIS STUDY IS CALLED GENEALOGY. IF YOU'D LIKE TO LEARN ABOUT YOUR OWN GENEALOGY AND HOW YOUR ANCESTORS CAME TO AMERICA, VISIT WWW.INAMERICABOOKS.COM FOR TIPS AND LINKS TO HELP YOU GET STARTED.

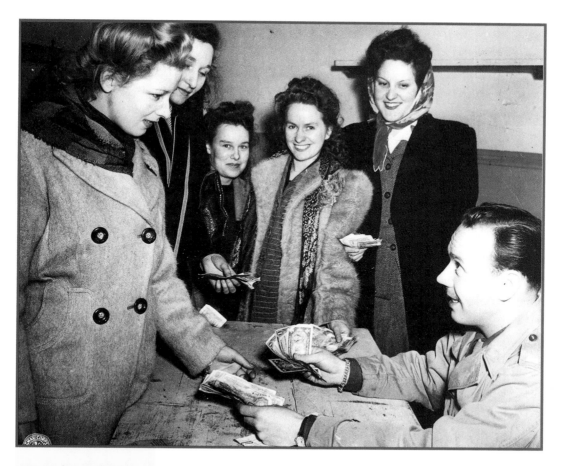

British war brides exchange British pounds for U.S. dollars before sailing to their new homes in the United States.

With their shared language and customs, it was natural for the United States and Britain to engage in cultural exchange in the twentieth century. For instance, in the 1950s, many British teenagers listened to American rock-and-roll musicians such as Elvis Presley and Buddy Holly. In the 1960s, American teenagers fell in love with the Beatles, the Rolling Stones, the Who, and other British bands (together known as the British Invasion).

British films and TV shows also became popular with Americans. One of the most famous was *Monty*

Python's Flying Circus, a sidesplitting TV comedy that played on U.S. as well as British stations in the 1970s. When Diana Spencer married Britain's Prince Charles in 1981, Americans went wild for the new princess. When Diana died in a car crash in 1997, Americans were grief stricken. Soon after, many Americans, especially young women, swooned over Diana and Charles's sons, the British princes William and Harry. Other Americans flocked to hear new British rock bands, such as Radiohead, Oasis, and Coldplay.

Throughout the twentieth century, British people continued to emigrate to the United States, although not in great numbers. They came to attend school, get married, or live closer to family.

Radiohead gained wide popularity in the United States after the release of their first studio album, Pablo Honey. *They continue to win accolades from fans and critics alike. In 2005* OK Computer, *their third release, was named the top album of the past twenty years by* Spin *magazine.*

This Jewish British American family looks at family photographs together.

Many felt that U.S. society offered more openness and tolerance than British society. Others loved the wide-open landscapes of the American West. Still others were attracted by job opportunities in the United States.

Ties between the United States and Great Britain remained strong. For instance, when the United States decided to go to war in Iraq in 2003, Britain joined in the fight. When terrorist bombs killed more than fifty people in London in 2005, the United States pledged its support to Britain. Both nations worked together to fight terrorism at home and around the world.

TROUBLE FOR TRAVELERS

Throughout the twentieth century, it was fairly easy for British people to travel and work in the United States. But on September 11, 2001, foreign terrorists attacked the United States. Afterward, the U.S. government tightened security at airports. The government also made it harder for foreigners to get visas and green cards—documents that allow foreign people to live, work, and travel in the United States. This situation created frustrations for British people, who were used to traveling freely between the two nations.

CELEBRATING THEIR ROOTS

In the twenty-first century, the British in America are still proud of their heritage. Many use the Internet to trace their ancestors back to Britain and then back through the generations in Britain. Heritage societies such as the Daughters of the American Revolution and the Sons of the American Revolution continue to thrive. Many people of Scottish heritage take part in the Highland Games. This event, held in many cities across the United States, features Scottish foods, dancing, costumes, and music, as well as traditional Scottish sporting events such as wrestling, tug-of-war, and the hammer toss. The games are especially popular in the South, where many Scottish immigrants settled in colonial days. At the yearly North American

In the hammer toss contest (above) *during the Highland Games, athletes throw a sixteen- or twenty-two-pound hammer as far as possible. Check out www.inamericabooks.com for links to locate British events and activities in your area.*

Festival of Wales, people come together to enjoy traditional Welsh foods, poetry, music, and crafts.

It's easy to celebrate British heritage in the United States. On the East Coast, many monuments and historic sites pay tribute to the first British colonists. People can visit the site of the original Jamestown settlement, the Plymouth Colony, a replica of the *Mayflower,* and other colonial-era attractions. A reality-style TV show called *Colonial House* shows firsthand what it was like to live in colonial New England. Living history museums such as Colonial Williamsburg also allow visitors to experience colonial life up close.

WELSH RAREBIT

Sometimes called Welsh rabbit, this traditional Welsh dish makes a tasty snack or breakfast food. The name rarebit comes from *rare,* meaning lightly cooked, and *bit,* meaning a small portion. To learn how to prepare other British Isles dishes, visit www.inamericabooks.com for links.

1½ CUPS GRATED CHEDDAR CHEESE

2 TABLESPOONS MILK

2 TABLESPOONS BUTTER

1 TEASPOON DIJON MUSTARD

1 PINCH PEPPER

2 SLICES BREAD

1. Place cheese, milk, butter, mustard, and pepper in a small saucepan. Cook on low heat, stirring continuously until mixture is thick and smooth.
2. Toast bread slices in a toaster.
3. Pour mixture over toasted bread.

Serves 2

CHECK OUT
WWW.INAMERICABOOKS.COM
FOR TIPS ON RESEARCHING
NAMES IN YOUR FAMILY
HISTORY.

But you don't have to go to a museum or historic site to see evidence of the British in America. The evidence is all around you. For instance, do you know someone with the last name Taylor or Weaver? Chances are that person has British ancestors. Have you ever been to Birmingham, Alabama? It was named for Birmingham, England. Belfast, Maine, was named for Belfast in Northern Ireland. English, the language you use every day, originated in Great Britain. The song "America" (sometimes called "My Country 'Tis of Thee") takes its tune from the national anthem of the United Kingdom. Do you like to eat roast beef or fish and chips? Those are traditional British foods. The British in America may no longer make up a large percentage of the U.S. population, but their influence is felt far and wide.

THE UNITED STATES IS THE MOST WELCOMING, OPEN, AND GENEROUS COUNTRY IN THE WORLD.

—*Jonathan Slator, twentieth-century British immigrant*

FAMOUS BRITISH AMERICANS

PIERS ANTHONY (b. 1934) Born Piers Anthony Dillingham Jacob in

Oxford, England, Anthony is a popular science fiction author. He moved with his family to the United States at the age of six. Anthony earned a bachelor's degree from Goddard College in Vermont in 1956 and served in the U.S. army from 1957 to 1959, during which time. he became a U.S. citizen. Anthony held a wide variety of jobs before his first novel, *Chthon*, was published in 1967. Since then he has published more than 100 works and has appeared on the *New York Times* bestseller list more than twenty times. Anthony's most popular novels are those in his Xanth series.

LANCE ARMSTRONG (b. 1971) Born in Plano, Texas, Lance Armstrong is a champion bicycle racer. He competed in triathlons as a boy and joined the Motorola bicycle racing team as a young man. In 1996 doctors discovered that Armstrong was sick with cancer. He underwent surgery and chemotherapy and was able to return to bicycle racing. Starting in 1999, Armstrong won the Tour de France—a famous, three-week-long bicycle race—seven years in a row. In addition to bicycle racing, Armstrong heads the Lance Armstrong Foundation, an organization dedicated to

fighting cancer and helping cancer patients. Armstrong is of Scottish descent.

ANNE BRADSTREET (ca. 1612–1672) Anne Bradstreet, a resident of the Massachusetts Bay Colony, published *The Tenth Muse Lately Sprung Up in America*, the first volume of poetry written in the American colonies. Historians think that Bradstreet was born in

Northampton, England. Her original name was Anne Dudley. She married Simon Bradstreet as a teenager and moved to Massachusetts in 1630. In her poetry, Bradstreet wrote about religious and moral ideas and colonial home life.

ANDREW CARNEGIE

(1835–1919) A wealthy manufacturer, Andrew Carnegie was born in Dunfermline, Scotland. As a boy, he moved with

his family to Pittsburgh, Pennsylvania. Carnegie began his career in the railroad industry, then entered the oil and steel businesses, which made him very rich. After his retirement, Carnegie gave away vast amounts of money to causes he believed in. He helped establish libraries, colleges, and other institutions, including Carnegie Hall in New York City.

KIT CARSON (1809–1868)

Christopher "Kit" Carson was a well-known U.S. soldier and frontiersman. His ancestors came

to America from Scotland. Carson was born in Madison County, Kentucky, but grew up in Missouri. Carson left home as a teenager and worked as a fur trapper and trader in the American West. He helped guide John C. Frémont's expedition to explore the West in the 1840s. He served in the Mexican American War (1846–1848) and the Civil War (1861–1865). Afterward, he led campaigns against Native Americans in the American West.

HILLARY CLINTON (b. 1947)

Senator Hillary Rodham Clinton was born in Chicago, Illinois, and grew up in the Chicago suburb of Park Ridge. She attended Wellesley College and then earned a law degree from Yale University. She moved to Fayetteville, Arkansas, where she worked as a lawyer and married Bill Clinton, who later became president of the

United States. As a lawyer and as First Lady, Clinton focused on issues of children's rights, fighting poverty, and improving health care for Americans. She also wrote several books. She was elected to the U.S. Senate from the state of New York in 2000. Clinton's ancestors are Welsh.

SHEENA EASTON (b. 1959) Pop

singer Easton was born Sheena Shirley Orr in Bellshill, Scotland. Her

most famous songs include the James Bond movie theme "For Your Eyes Only" and "U Got the Look," a duet she sang with Prince. A two-time Grammy Award winner (Best New Artist in 1981 and Best Mexican American Performance for the song "Me Gustas Tal Como Eres" in 1984), Easton has also worked in film, television, and on Broadway. She became a U.S. citizen in 1992.

BENJAMIN FRANKLIN

(1706–1790) Born in Boston, Massachusetts, Benjamin Franklin was a great colonial statesman, writer, publisher, inventor, and scientist. He was descended from English immigrants to North America. Largely self-educated, Franklin excelled in many fields. As a writer and publisher, he was most famous for creating *Poor Richard's Almanac.*

As a scientist, he invented the lightning rod, the Franklin stove, and bifocal eyeglasses, and he proved that lightning is electricity. Franklin was very active in the government of colonial Philadelphia. He also served as postmaster for the American colonies, a member of the Second Continental Congress, a signer of the Declaration of Independence, and a U.S. ambassador to France.

BILL GATES (b.

1955) Cofounder and chairman of the Microsoft Corporation, William (Bill) Gates is one of the

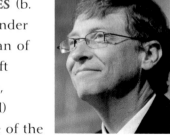

world's most successful businesspeople. Gates was born in Seattle, Washington. In 1970, at the age of fifteen, he created a computer software company with his friend Paul Allen. In 1975 the two young men founded Microsoft and developed the Microsoft Disk Operating System (MS–DOS). Since its founding, Microsoft has grown to dominate the computer software industry. Bill Gates and his wife, Melinda, started the Gates Foundation in 1999. Gates uses the foundation to fund health–care and educational programs around the world. His ancestors on his mother's side are Scottish.

ALFRED HITCHCOCK

(1899–1980) Movie director Alfred Hitchcock was born in London, England. He began making films in Great Britain in the 1920s. In 1939 he moved to the United States and became a U.S. citizen. He worked in Hollywood, becoming famous for making suspense thrillers. His best–known works include *Strangers on a Train* (1951), *The Man Who Knew*

Too Much (1956), *North by Northwest* (1959), and *Psycho* (1960). Hitchcock also hosted a television series in the 1950s and 1960s.

CHRISTOPHER HITCHENS (b. 1949)

Hitchens is well known for his books and articles on political topics. Born in Portsmouth, England, Hitchens attended the prestigious University of Oxford, where he studied philosophy, politics, and economics. He worked for newspapers in London before moving to the United States in the early 1980s. Hitchens's work has appeared in

the *Nation*, *Harper's*, the *Los Angeles Times Book Review*, *Vanity Fair*, *Slate*, the *New York Review of Books*, the *Washington Post*, the *Atlantic Monthly*, and other publications. He has also written more than ten books on politics and culture. He lives in Washington, D.C.

DAVID HOCKNEY (b. 1937)

Hockney is a famed British American painter, photographer, and printmaker. Born in Bradford, England, Hockney studied art at the Royal College of Art in London. He emerged as a leader of the British pop art movement in the early 1960s, then moved to

Los Angeles, California, in 1963. Hockney often incorporates photographs and collages into his paintings. Some of his most famous works show scenes of blue skies, swimming pools, and the sunny Southern California lifestyle.

ANTHONY HOPKINS (b. 1937)

Acclaimed actor Anthony Hopkins was born in Port Talbot, Wales. As a young man, he studied acting at the

Royal Academy of Dramatic Art in London. Hopkins worked as a stage actor in both London and New York City, then began making Hollywood films. He has appeared in almost one hundred movies, including *Silence of the Lambs, Nixon,* and *Amistad.* His *Silence of the Lambs* performance earned him an Oscar for best actor in 1992. Hopkins became a U.S. citizen in 2000.

JULIA WARD HOWE

(1819–1910) Howe, born into a wealthy New York City family, has had a lasting affect on U.S. culture. As a young woman, she moved to Boston, where she became active in the antislavery movement. During the Civil War, she wrote the words to "The Battle Hymn of the Republic," a dramatic, patriotic song. After the war, Howe became involved in the movement for woman's rights and suffrage (the right to vote). In 1872 she proposed

the idea for Mother's Day. Gradually, others picked up on her idea, and Mother's Day won national recognition in 1914. Howe had English ancestors.

THOMAS JEFFERSON

(1743–1826) The third president of the United States, Jefferson was born in present–day Albemarle County, Virginia. He attended the College of William and Mary and began his career as a lawyer. In 1769 he joined Virginia's colonial legislature.

He also joined the movement for American independence and wrote the Declaration of Independence in 1776. After the Revolutionary War, Jefferson served as a U.S. Congress member, minister to France, secretary of state, vice president, and president. During his presidency, he helped the young United States grow stronger and larger, especially with the 1803 Louisiana Purchase. Jefferson was also a noted inventor, philosopher, and farmer. His ancestors were Welsh.

BILLIE JEAN KING (b. 1943)

Born in Long Beach, California,

Billie Jean Moffitt King made her fame as a top tennis player in the 1960s and 1970s. In 1972 *Sports Illustrated* magazine named her Sportsperson of the Year—the first woman given that honor. In 1973 King convinced other female tennis players to form a union, the Women's Tennis Association, which led to much higher pay and prize money for women in professional tennis. In 1974 King founded the Women's Sports Foundation, dedicated to improving opportunities for women in sports. After retiring from tennis, King became a coach, TV announcer, and writer. Her ancestors were Scottish.

BARBARA MCCLINTOCK

(1902–1992) McClintock, a Scottish

American, won the 1983 Nobel Prize in Physiology—a branch of science that deals with the function of living things. McClintock was born in Hartford, Connecticut. She attended Cornell University as an undergraduate and a graduate student, earning a Ph.D. from the university in 1927. Working at Cornell, the University of Missouri, and the Carnegie Institute, McClintock studied genetic mutations, or changes, in corn plants. Her discoveries led other researchers to a better understanding of the role of genes in human disease.

JOHN MUIR (1838–1914)

Naturalist John Muir was born in Dunbar, Scotland. He moved with

his family to Wisconsin at the age of eleven. As a young man, he enrolled at the University of Wisconsin, where he studied the natural sciences. In 1868 Muir set out to explore North America. He traveled on foot, visiting then little–known parts of California, Alaska, and other regions. He also traveled in Europe, Asia, and Africa. In 1892 Muir founded the Sierra Club, a famous conservation society. Muir also authored several books about the American wilderness and conservation. His work helped convince the U.S. government to set aside thousands of acres of land as national parks and national forests.

EDGAR ALLAN POE (1809–1849)

A poet, short–story writer, and

literary critic, Edgar Allan Poe was born in Boston, Massachusetts. His ancestors were Scots–Irish. As a young man, Poe traveled, studied at the University of Virginia, and served in the U.S. Army. He published his first book of poetry in 1827 and continued writing until his death. His works are famous for being dark, dramatic, and spooky. Some of Poe's best–known works are "The Murders in the Rue Morgue" (a short story) and "The Raven" (a poem).

MARK TWAIN (1835–1910)

Mark Twain was the pen (fictitious) name of Samuel Langhorne Clemens. Clemens was born in Florida, Missouri, and grew up in Hannibal, Missouri, a town

on the Mississippi River. He worked as a riverboat pilot and a newspaper reporter as a young man. While writing for the *Territorial Enterprise*, a Nevada newspaper, he took the name Mark Twain, a riverboat term. Twain's literary works include novels, travel stories, short stories, and essays. His most well–known books include *The Adventures of Tom Sawyer*, *The Adventures of Huckleberry Finn*, *Innocents Abroad*, *The Prince and the Pauper,* and *A Connecticut Yankee in King Arthur's Court.* His ancestors were English.

FRANK LLOYD WRIGHT

(1867–1959) Born in Richland Center, Wisconsin, Frank Lloyd Wright was a world–famous U.S. architect. His ancestors were Welsh. As a young man, Wright briefly studied engineering at the University of Wisconsin. He then moved to Chicago, where he worked for several architectural firms before opening his own architectural business. Wright is known for many striking and innovative works, such as his prairie–style homes that

artfully blend indoor and outdoor spaces. Other famous works include the Robie House in Illinois, the Fallingwater (a house in Pennsylvania), and the Johnson Wax Company building in Wisconsin.

TIMELINE

ca. 500 B.C.	Celtic people from France arrive in the British Isles.
55 B.C.	Roman troops invade the British Isles.
A.D. 400s	Patrick converts the Irish Celts to Christianity.
late 500s	Augustine converts the Anglo-Saxons to Christianity.
1066	William defeats King Harold at the Battle of Hastings.
1284	England takes over Wales.
1492	Christopher Columbus lands in the West Indies.
1606	Wealthy Englishmen form the London Company.
1607	Settlers arrive at Jamestown in Virginia.
1620	Puritan Separatists and other colonists arrive in Plymouth, Massachusetts.
1629	The Great Migration of Puritans begins.
1642	William Berkeley becomes the royal governor of Virginia. Civil war begins in Britain.
1682	William Penn establishes Pennsylvania.
1717	Parliament begins sending convicted felons to the American colonies.
1754–1763	Britain and France fight the French and Indian War in North America.
1775–1783	American colonists fight the Revolutionary War for independence from Britain.
1803	The United States buys more than eight hundred thousand square miles of land from France in a deal called the Louisiana Purchase.

1890	Anglo–American women found the Daughters of the American Revolution.
1897	Descendants of the Pilgrims found the Mayflower Society.
1917	The United States assists Britain and its allies in World War I.
1941–1945	The United States assists Britain and its allies in World War II.
1964	The Beatles make their first trip to the United States, kicking off the "British Invasion."
1981	Prince Charles marries Diana Spencer.
1997	Princess Diana dies in a car crash in France.
2001	Terrorists attack targets in the United States. The United States tightens security at airports, causing difficulties for British and other foreign travelers.
2003	Britain assists the United States in the Iraq war.
2005	Terrorists bomb subways and buses in London.

GLOSSARY

BACKCOUNTRY: a remote, undeveloped rural area

BRITAIN: the island encompassing England, Scotland, and Wales; also called Great Britain

COLONY: a group of people living in a new territory but maintaining ties with their home territory

DISSENTER: someone who disagrees with accepted teachings

EMIGRANT: a person who leaves his or her homeland to live somewhere else

IMMIGRANT: a person who enters a country to make his or her home there

INDENTURED SERVANT: a person who agrees to labor for a certain amount of time in exchange for travel expenses, food, clothing, and housing

INDIAN: a Native American

LEGISLATURE: a group of people with the power to make laws

MISSIONARY: a person who tries to convert others to his or her religion

PARLIAMENT: the British legislature

PERSECUTION: harassment, discrimination, or punishment, often carried out against people of a specific religious, ethnic, or racial group

PLANTATION: a large farm

PROTESTANT: a member of a non-Catholic Christian church

TENANT FARMER: a farmer who works land owned by someone else and pays rent in either money or crops

UNITED KINGDOM: the present-day nation encompassing England, Scotland, Wales, and Northern Ireland

THINGS TO SEE AND DO

COLONIAL NATIONAL HISTORIC
PARK, YORKTOWN, VIRGINIA
http://www.nps.gov/colo/home.htm
Run by the National Park Service,
this attraction encompasses several
historic sites, including the
Jamestown settlement and
Yorktown, the site of the last battle
of the American Revolution. In
between, visitors can drive the
twenty-three-mile Colonial Parkway.

COLONIAL WILLIAMSBURG,
WILLIAMSBURG, VIRGINIA
http://www.history.org
This famous living history museum
gives visitors an up close look at
colonial America life. Guides dress
in period costumes, demonstrate
colonial-era crafts, and play
authentic music from colonial times.
Visitors can tour museums and
colonial-era buildings and take part
in many educational programs.

GRANDFATHER MOUNTAIN
HIGHLAND GAMES, LINVILLE,
NORTH CAROLINA
http://www.gmhg.org
The Grandfather Mountain Highland
Games is a yearly gathering of
thousands of Scottish Americans.

The celebration includes Scottish
fiddling, piping, and dancing;
traditional sporting events such as
wrestling; Scottish foods; and even
traditional activities such as
sheepherding. Many participants
gather with other people of the
same clan—or large family group
originating in Scotland.

PLIMOTH PLANTATION, PLYMOUTH,
MASSACHUSETTS
http://plimoth.org
Plimoth Plantation re-creates
Plymouth Colony as it looked in the
1600s. Visitors can tour the 1627
Pilgrim village, a Native American
village called Hobbamock's
Homesite, the *Mayflower II* (a replica
of the original *Mayflower*), and much
more. Guides in period costumes
help bring the site to life.

SALEM WITCH MUSEUM, SALEM,
MASSACHUSETTS
http://www.salemwitchmuseum.com
Using lifelike displays and historic
artifacts, the museum tells the story
of the 1692 witch hunt in Salem. A
special exhibit examines perceptions
of witches and witchcraft through
history.

SOURCE NOTES

17 David Hackett Fischer, *Albion's Seed: Four British Folkways in America* (New York: Oxford University Press, 1989), 250.

18 C. H. Firth, ed., *An American Garland: Being a Collection of Ballads Relating to America, 1563–1759* (1915; repr., Detroit: Singing Tree Press, 1969), 47.

21 Firth, xxiv.

24 Fischer, 18, 20.

25 Firth, 27.

35 Alan Taylor, *American Colonies: The Settling of North America* (New York: Penguin Books, 2001), 266.

36 Firth, xxvi–xxvii.

36 Firth, 44.

40 Fischer, 605.

50 Eric Richards, *Britannia's Children: Emigration from England, Scotland, Wales, and Ireland Since 1600* (London: Hambledon and London, 2004), 5.

55 Hugh Elliot, interview with author, June 2, 2005.

59 Jonathan Slator, interview with author, July 2, 2005.

SELECTED BIBLIOGRAPHY

Firth, C. H., ed. *An American Garland: Being a Collection of Ballads Relating to America 1563–1759.* 1915. Reprint, Detroit: Singing Tree Press, 1969. During the major years of British migration to America, songwriters created ballads that told the migrants' stories. Some ballads sang the praises of Virginia or New England— usually to promote settlement. Others described the religious oppression that led people to leave Britain. Still others chronicled the hardships of the voyage and settlement in North America. This book contains the words to twenty-five songs, along with scholarly commentary.

Fischer, David Hackett. *Albion's Seed: Four British Folkways in America.* New York: Oxford University Press, 1989. Fischer looks at four major waves of British migration—to New England, Virginia, Pennsylvania, and the American backcountry (frontier). For each group of migrants, he details their lives and origins in Britain and then shows how their folkways survived in America.

Fry, Michael. *How the Scots Made America.* New York: Thomas Dunne Books, 2003. Fry describes the experiences of the early Scottish immigrants in America. He then tells the stories of famous Americans who can trace their ancestors to Scotland, including presidents, businesspeople, and entertainers.

Hofstadter, Richard. *America at 1750: A Social Portrait.* New York: Alfred A. Knopf, 1971. The author examines the lives of indentured servants, slaves, and other common people in colonial America. He also explores social, religious, and cultural aspects of colonial society.

Quinn, Arthur. *A New World: An Epic of Colonial America from the Founding of Jamestown to the Fall of Quebec.* New York: Berkley Books, 1994. Quinn chronicles both British and French efforts to colonize North America. He explores the various religious and economic forces that drove people to migrate to America and shows how different groups struggled, thrived, and interacted with one another in the New World.

Ray, Celeste. *Highland Heritage: Scottish Americans in the American South.* Chapel Hill: University of North Carolina Press, 2001. Almost five million Americans claim to have at least one Scottish ancestor. Another four million boast Scots-Irish ancestry. Many of these Americans participate in the Highland Games, clan gatherings, and other heritage events. This scholarly work examines Scottish American identity and the sometimes romanticized view of Scottish heritage.

Richards, Eric. *Britannia's Children: Emigration from England, Scotland, Wales, and Ireland Since 1600.* London: Hambledon and London, 2004.

British emigrants did not just settle on the North American mainland. They also moved to the West Indies, Australia, New Zealand, South Africa, and elsewhere. This book examines the entire British migration, from 1600 to the late 1900s. Several chapters deal exclusively with migration to America.

Taylor, Alan. *American Colonies: The Settling of North America.* New York: Penguin Books, 2001. This comprehensive work details the European colonization of America from the late 1400s to the early 1800s. The author describes the life of Native Americans, the European migration to different regions of North America, and the creation and growth of the young United States.

FURTHER READING & WEBSITES

NONFICTION

Aronson, Marc. *John Winthrop, Oliver Cromwell, and the Land of Promise.* New York: Clarion Books, 2004. In this thoroughly researched and well-illustrated book for young people, the author examines the political and religious climate in Britain that led to the creation of the Massachusetts Bay Colony and other British colonies in America.

Campbell, Kumari. *United Kingdom in Pictures*. Minneapolis: Lerner Publications Company, 2004. The British colonies in America were made up largely of settlers from England, Wales, Scotland, and Northern Ireland—the present-day nation called the United Kingdom. This title explores that nation's history, culture, economy, and more.

Day, Nancy. *Your Travel Guide to Colonial America*. Minneapolis: Lerner Publications Company, 2001. This fun-filled and fact-filled title takes readers back in time to Jamestown, Plymouth, and other colonial settlements. Readers will learn about daily life in the colonies, famous colonists, and much more.

McPherson, Stephanie Sammartino. *Sir Walter Raleigh*. Minneapolis: Lerner Publications Company, 2005. A favorite of Queen Elizabeth, Raleigh explored the New World and attempted to set up American colonies for Great Britain. This book tells the story of his life.

Miller, Brandon Marie. *Good Women of a Well-Blessed Land: Women's Lives in Colonial America*. Minneapolis: Lerner Publications Company, 2003. Drawing on diaries, letters, and other primary sources, this in-depth history offers insight into the lives of female colonists, as well as African and native women in colonial America.

——. *Growing Up in a New World: 1607 to 1775*. Minneapolis: Lerner Publications Company, 2003. A large percentage of the British colonists in North America were children. Using historical documents and other primary sources, Miller examines the lives of colonial children and the hardships they faced in the New World.

Swain, Gwenyth. *Freedom Seeker: A Story about William Penn*. Minneapolis: Carolrhoda Books, Inc., 2003. William Penn led the Quaker migration to America. He founded the Pennsylvania colony, where everyone was allowed to worship freely. This book tells his story.

Wilson, Lori Lee. *The Salem Witch Trials*. Minneapolis: Twenty-First Century Books, 1997. Wilson examines the Salem witch trials through engaging text and primary source materials.

FICTION

Cooper, James Fenimore. *The Leatherstocking Tales I: The Pioneers, The Last of the Mohicans, The Prairie.* New York: Library of America, 1985.

———. *The Leatherstocking Tales II: The Pathfinder, The Deerslayer.* New York: Library of America, 1985. Cooper's five classic novels take an action-packed look at eighteenth-century America. The books follow the adventures of Natty Bumppo, a frontiersman in upstate New York. The books also examine the clash between Native American civilization and advancing white society in North America.

Kelly, Nancy. *The Whisper Rod: A Tale of Old Massachusetts.* Shippensburg, PA: White Mane Publishing Company, 2001. Fourteen-year-old Hannah Pryor lives in colonial Boston, where Quakers are not allowed to practice their faith. Witnessing the harsh persecution of Quakers, Hannah must reconsider her own Puritan upbringing and beliefs.

Rinaldi, Ann. *A Break with Charity: A Story about the Salem Witch Trials.* San Diego: Gulliver Books, 2003. A blend of fictional characters and historical fact, this novel for young adults tells the story of the Salem witch trials from the perspective of fourteen-year-old Susannah English.

———. *The Journal of Jasper Jonathan Pierce, a Pilgrim Boy.* New York: Scholastic Inc., 2000. Rinaldi explores the experiences of Jasper Pierce, a fourteen-year-old indentured servant sent to America aboard the Mayflower. Although Jasper is a fictional character, Rinaldi surrounds him with true historical characters and events.

WEBSITES

DoHistory
http://dohistory.org
This site shows young people how to explore history for themselves. It focuses on Martha Ballard, a colonial Massachusetts midwife, and shows how historians and nonhistorians can use Ballard's diary to learn more about life in colonial America.

INAMERICABOOKS.COM
http://www.inamericabooks.com
Visit inamericabooks.com, the online home of the In America series, to get linked to all sorts of useful information. You'll find historical and cultural websites related to individual groups, as well as general information on genealogy, creating your own family tree, and the history of immigration in America.

MAYFLOWERHISTORY.COM
http://www.mayflowerhistory.com
This site offers a wealth of information on the Mayflower, including a list of passengers, historical texts, and extensive links to other sites.

VIRTUAL JAMESTOWN
http://virtualjamestown.org
This site is loaded with primary materials, such as maps, public documents, and correspondence from Jamestown colonists. The material sheds much light on the experiences of the Jamestown settlers.

INDEX

ACKNOWLEDGMENTS: THE PHOTOGRAPHS IN THIS BOOK ARE REPRODUCED WITH THE PERMISSION OF: Digital Vision Royalty Free, pp. 1, 3, 22; © PoodlesRock/CORBIS, p. 6; Library of Congress, pp. 7 (LC–DIG–ppmsc–07996), 30 (LC–USZ62–78099), 32 (LC–USZ62–29058), 48 (LC–USZc4–4971), 60 (bottom right, PS–712–C25RBD Rare book division), 61 (left), 62 (top right, LC–USZC4–7214), 64 (top right, LC–USZ62–4820), 66 (top left, LC–USZ62–25974; right, LC–USZ62–112065 © A.F. Bradley, New York); © North Wind Picture Archives, pp. 8, 11, 15, 21, 24, 27, 29, 45; © Brown Brothers, pp. 10, 16, 53; The Granger Collection, New York, pp. 12, 13, 44; The Library of Virginia, p. 17; Mary Evans Picture Library, p. 19; © Stock Montage, Inc., p. 34; The Pennsylvania Academy of the Fine Arts, p. 37; Union Pacific Historical Collection, p. 51; © Justin Borucki/Retna Ltd., p. 54; © Erica Johnson/Independent Picture Service, p. 55; © P. TOMKINS/VisitScotland/SCOTTISH VIEWPOINT, p. 57; Courtesy Carol Ann Marble, p. 60 (left); © Alexandre Marchi/Maxppp/ZUMA Press, p. 60 (top right); Starsmore Center for Local History, Colorado Springs Pioneers Museum, p. 61 (top right); Hillary Rodham Clinton, Office of the Senator, p. 61 (bottom right); © Denis O'Regan/CORBIS, p. 62 (left); © Chris Kleponis/ZUMA Press, p. 62 (bottom right); Hollywood Book and Poster, p. 63 (left); © Gene Blevins/CORBIS, p. 63 (right); © UPPA/ZUMA Press, p. 64 (top left); © Lisa O'Connor/ZUMA Press, p. 64 (bottom left); Independence National Historical Park, p. 64 (bottom right); HBO Sports/TEAMTENNIS, p. 65 (left); © AP/Wide World Photos, p. 65 (right); Harris Collection of American Poetry and Plays, Brown University Library, p. 66 (bottom left); Frank Lloyd Wright Preservation Trust, Negative #H273, p. 67; Maps by Bill Hauser, pp. 14, 47.

Front Cover: Library of Congress (top, LC–USZ62–118128); Digital Vision Royalty Free (title); © PoodlesRock/CORBIS (bottom). Back Cover: Digital Vision Royalty Free.